GOATED BY THE GODS

SHERI LYN

Copyright

This book is a work of fiction. The names, characters, places, and incidents are fictitious or have been used fictitiously, and are not to be construed as real in any way. Any resemblance to persons, living or dead, actual events, locales, or organizations is entirely coincidental.

Published By

Gae Gae Press

Palm Harbor, Fl 34685

http://www.sherilynauthor.com/

Goated By The Gods

Copyright © 2016 by Sheri Lyn

Cover by Ash Arceneaux

All Rights Are Reserved. No part of this book may be used or reproduced in any manner whatsoever without written permission, except in the case of brief quotations embodied in critical articles and reviews.

Property of Sheri Lyn

May 2016

Dedication

To everyone who has a dream that one day they will find their other half. I hope the Gods and Goddesses help guide you on the journey to everlasting love.

To Koda, the love of my life. You have brought me happiness and unconditional love. Without you, I don't know if I would have made it. I wish I could keep you by myside forever.

One

Zach surveyed the young faces that surrounded the campfire and smiled contentedly. These kids didn't get to do many fun things in their lives and he and his brothers were happy to help in any way they could. The best thing they had ever done was start this camp for kids like them.

Tomorrow they would head back to the orphanage they lived in and with any luck, have good memories to hold them over for a time.

"We have time for one more story, gang, then it's time for bed. We have to leave early tomorrow to catch the bus back home," one of the counselors announced with a stern look at the faces of the kids staring up at her.

"Mr. Zach, will you tell us the last story, please?" a young voice piped up eagerly, a round of agreements echoing the plea.

Zach glanced around the campfire at the expectant faces and the smirking ones of his brothers.

"How many of you have heard tales of the gods?" He glanced around, waiting for anyone to respond, then with a sigh he continued.

"There is an old myth that my family likes to pass on. I will tell it to you, but then you must agree to go to bed without fuss for your counselors. Agreed?"

A chorus of "Yes, sir" filled the air.

"Good, now the story begins with the god Thor, who drives a chariot through the sky." Zach paused and glanced to the child dancing in his seat with excitement. Did he have to pee? Was he bored? What the hell did the kid want already? Zach glanced to the counselors with a look of alarm flashing across his face.

"Did you have a question, Michael?" the counselor asked with a smile on her face.

"Yes, Ms. Jackie, I do. What is a chariot?"

"Oh, um, yeah, sorry. A chariot is like a wheeled bucket type thing that horses, or in Thor's case goats pull. Does that make sense to you guys?"

The kids gave a chorus of "Yes" and nods of agreements.

Zach cleared his throat and continued on with the story. "Each night, Thor would kill, cook and eat the goats, all but the bones. When he was finished eating, he'd take the bones and wrap them in cloth and in the morning the goats would be reborn to pull his chariot again."

Zach took a breath and let it out in a rush. He always hated this next part. The stupidity of one kid had doomed the whole family for eternity.

"One night, Thor stopped at a peasant, um, poor farmer's home and offered to share his goat meal with them in exchange for staying the night. During the meal, the poor farmer's son broke one of the goat's bones to get the marrow or, um, meat from inside. The next morning when the goats came back to life, one of them had a broken leg. In anger, Thor cursed the poor farming family to walk the earth as shapeshifters. They were men and goats."

"Why is that a curse? Wouldn't it be cool to be able to be a goat and a man?" Michael asked uncertainly.

"It would have its benefits, that's true, but could you imagine telling a girl or boy you liked that you were part goat?" Zach waited for their laughter and snickers to die down before he continued. "All right, gang, that's it. Off to bed with you, and I hope you had fun this week."

The brothers sat alone by the fire, listening to the cracks and pops of the glowing embers. "You know I hate when you tell that story, but you still do it every time," Quentin grunted out.

"I sure do, and that's just one of the reason's I tell it," Zach replied

"Knock it off, you two. Now isn't the time to fight over what can't be changed. We are what we are. The gods know we have tried to undo that damn curse. Thor is as stubborn as the day is long. Besides, you were right, Zach, there are some benefits to this crap," Jared tossed out with a smirk.

"Yeah, like what?" Zach asked belligerently.

"There isn't much we can't climb, which has saved how many lives since we joined the rescue crew?" Jared said as he walked away from the warmth of the fire.

Two

Thor looked down upon the Isle of Man and contemplated his past actions. He hadn't meant to let the curse go for so long, but things kept coming up and before he knew it, the years on earth had passed swiftly. He sometimes forgot how short human lives were; when you were immortal, time had little value. He desperately wanted to make amends with the farmer's family for spiting them. Especially when in all honesty, he had healed the goat's leg with his powers. He just needed to let his anger cool down, as they say, and the next thing he knew it had been a couple thousand years.

"Have you figured out what you are going to do yet?" Thor's wife, Sif, asked as she approached him.

"I have been watching the farmer's descendants and can't in good faith take away their 'curse,' for look what they have done with it. They save countless lives because of their abilities. The goat is a mighty animal. There are only a few things it can't climb, and they are natural escape artists. No, I can't take the curse away, but perhaps I can make it up to them."

Sif's laughter filled the space, "And just how do you propose to do that?"

"Why, wife, I shall find them their mates. What better way to make them happy than to give them the other half of their hearts?"

She scoffed at his ridiculous suggestion, "Again I ask, how do you propose to do that? You have no abilities to discover their mates, unless you have been hiding something from me."

"Simple, my arrogant wife, I will ask Freyja for help. She is the goddess of love after all. She must be able to help me in this matter."

"Oh, do please summon her, I can't wait to see how this goes."

"I am not Odin to be obeyed, I can't just summon her. But I did save her from two different marriage proposals to unworthy beings. The least she can do is assist me in this matter."

Thor looked up to see Freyja approaching them with a look of impatience on her face. "Well, look who has graced us with her presence."

"Tell me what it is you wish of me. I could hear you from a mile away blathering on and on and it became bothersome," Freyja said

"I need to right a wrong I committed many years ago, and I need your help."

"What service could I provide the great Thor?"

"Help me find the true mates of the sons of the farmer I cursed. You are a goddess of lust and love, surely you can discover their mates."

"I could, but why should I help you? What do I get in return?"

"What do you want? There are no battles we fight like we used to, the world has become complacent to our existence. How about in return for the gifts I gave you so long ago, of your most beloved blue cats that pull your chariot through the sky?"

"Fine, who is it?" Thor pointed the brothers out and watched in silence as Freyja examined the men. He wasn't sure how long this would take, but his excitement grew as her laughter filled the room.

"Oh, this is going to be fun." She pointed, "His mate is right under his nose and he doesn't have a clue. Wonder how he feels about half-bloods? His mate is a half-troll who has become something of a recluse. He spends a lot of his time in those very mountains the brothers climb and his name is Gareth. When I locate the others, I will let you know. In the meantime, have fun."

Freyja turned and walked away in a huff of impatience, mumbling under her breath about gifts not being worth the trouble.

"What has you smirking, Thor?" Loki asked as he walked up to stand beside them.

"Loki, my friend, how would you like to have some fun?"

"You know I am always up for causing some mischief, I mean some fun."

Thor laughed and returned his attention to the mortal realm once more. "Soon, my boys, you shall have your heart's desire, whether you are ready or not."

Three

"Quentin, Jared, let's go. We got a call for a missing hiker," Zach hollered down to his brothers.

Zach moved to the front hall closet, grabbed his gear and pulled his brother's gear out. "Thanks," Jared said as he picked his up, running for the jeep to get it packed and ready to go. Zach turned to look for Quentin, who was nowhere in sight. "Quent, let's go. Time is of the essence, man."

Quentin came running from the office. "Sorry, I'm ready. Let's go," he said as he barreled past Zach.

The three men stowed their gear and climbed in their four-wheel drive jeep. "What do we know?" Jared asked as he started the vehicle.

"Hiker left word at the ranger station he would be back yesterday. They lost contact with him about midday and haven't been able to ping his GPS since. Bad storms are moving in so they put a call out," Zach recited from the phone call he had received.

"Where was his last known location?" Quentin questioned.

Zach grimaced, "That's the tricky part. His last radio transmission reported that he was on Devil's Peak. They don't know if that was a mistake and his GPS was giving off false readings or if the guy was that far off course. They had spoken to the hiker every day and he was on the course he had laid out at the ranger station. There were even hikers who returned who said they had seen him on that trail."

"I'm confused. Why did they call us if they don't think he is on Devil's Peak?" Jared asked.

"They are sending their crew out to check the trail and different areas that way. On the off chance he is somehow on Devil's Peak, they called us in. We are the best and they know it. Have you guys been watching the radar? We have a limited amount of time before that snowstorm comes in. If this guy is still up there and it hits, he won't survive."

The three men grew quiet at Zach's words. They, better than most, knew how treacherous that terrain was. If they hadn't been part goat, they wouldn't be able to climb that mountain in the best of weather.

Silence filled the jeep as the men drove to the base of operations at the entrance to the park. They had to be mentally and physically prepared for what they would face up there. Yes, they had the advantage with their shifter abilities, but nothing was ever foolproof.

Zach was pulled from his thoughts when they reached their destination. He hated that people got lost in the mountains and he and his brothers were called in, but he loved being outdoors. He climbed out of the jeep and took a deep breath of the fresh, clean air. The smell of the trees and dirt, the cool wind blowing and the beautiful sunlight dappling through the trees almost made it seem like heaven on earth. If only they weren't here because someone was in danger.

"Let's check in with Mack and get our assignment before we unload," Zach called out to his brothers.

They made their way to where a group of men and women stood assembled in a circle. He knew all of them by sight and some of them by name. He and his brothers weren't part of the regular crew, but they had been called in enough to be recognized and acknowledged. "Welcome, boys. It's always a pleasure to see you, just wish it wasn't under these circumstances," Mack called out.

"Now that we all are here we can begin the debriefing. We have a male, approximately thirty-five years of age. He is an experienced hiker and amateur climber. He left word a week ago at the ranger station that he would be back yesterday morning. He made arrangements to check in via his satellite phone once a day to let them know his progress and if he had any issues arise. He failed to check in or show up as he had scheduled. We have hikers who reported seeing him along the trail and everything was fine they stated."

Mack sighed and rubbed a hand down his face in exhaustion. "His last transmission is what has us confused. His GPS coordinates have him high on Devil's Peak, but the day before he was over sixty-five miles in the opposite direction. "

"What is our instructions then? How are we handling this?" one of the rescuers asked.

"We are going to concentrate on the trail we know he was on. The Maddux brothers are here because they can safely and quickly get to Devil's Peak and check it out for us. I don't think our hiker is there, but I can't afford not to check it out." Mack nodded his head at Quentin's raised hand. "What's on your mind, son?"

"It seems pretty farfetched that based on one set of GPS coordinates, you are sending us to the mountain. Is there something you aren't telling us?"

"We received a call from a local plane flying overhead who said he was relaying a mayday call from the mountain. We know from past experience that the reception up there makes it practically impossible to send out signals. The pilot also reports seeing smoke for a moment. The odd thing about all of it is that it only lasted for about two minutes and it all disappeared.

The signal we could understand, but the smoke was just gone and the pilot couldn't find a trace of it at all, not even a plume in the sky above like if it had been doused." Mack groaned and looked away. "I know this sounds insane, but we have to check it out. I don't want to send a whole team up there for what could be a wild goose chase. I won't be able to sleep without checking it out either though. You boys can do it and get back in one piece, you have proven that time and time again."

Zach nodded his head in understanding and turned to get his gear from the jeep. It didn't matter if it sounded crazy or not, they had to check it out. For that matter, who would believe people could shift into goats? With the gods, the brothers knew nothing was impossible.

Quentin and Jared walked up and rifled through their bags, double-checking that everything was in order and nothing was missing.

"Ya'll ready for this?" Jared asked with a hint of excitement in his voice. Zach couldn't help but smile. Being out in the forest and the mountains with his brothers was one of his favorite things in the world to do.

"Let's hit it. If we hoof it, we can make it to the base of the mountain by dark," Jared responded.

"Really, you are such a dipshit. Did you have to say it like that?" Zach groused out.

The brothers laughed at his disgruntled tone. It didn't take much to rile him these days. They grabbed their gear, checked in with Mack and then headed out.

Four

Loki sat back against the cave wall and watched the fire crackle. Too bad Thor wasn't here to enjoy the lack of view. The next time he saw Thor, he was going to throw him off the side of the mountain. What was supposed to be fun and meant to stir up some excitement in his dull days had turned into a circus. This oaf of a man wouldn't let him leave the cave, and he didn't care what Loki had to say about it either. Damn shame he couldn't reveal his true self to the idiot, but a promise was a promise. Loki looked his captor over and had to admit for being half troll, he wasn't bad looking. He expected him to be hideous and ugly. Instead, he found Gareth to be rather striking with his dark blonde hair and rough mountain man beard. Okay, so it wasn't a beard per se, but it was stubble and it looked damn good on him. Gareth had to be about six four and packed some muscle. He had carried Loki as if he weighed nothing. It still boggled his mind to even think about it.

"I told you I could walk, you didn't have to carry me, you know," Loki ground out between clenched teeth. The indignity he had suffered for Thor.

"You shouldn't walk on that leg until you know if it's broken. Just sit tight and relax. I'll get you some food and you can hide here until the storm lets up."

"What storm?"

"The one that is going to hit shortly after daybreak tomorrow. You are lucky I was up here or you would be in serious danger of death."

Loki narrowed his eyes at the being in front of him. What was going on here, was he being played for a fool? Did the other gods set him up for a laugh?

"What's your name and why were you up here anyway?" Loki asked in suspicion

"I spend a lot of time up in these mountains. You could say it's a family tradition of sorts. I don't like being around a lot of people so I come up here to rejuvenate."

"Is that why there are so many, what do you call it...um, comforts?"

Gareth barked out a laugh. "Comforts, you say. Not many people would call this comfortable, but it works for me."

Loki looked around the small cave and would almost call it homey, well, at least it was for a troll.

"What's your name, anyway?" Gareth asked as he threw a stick on the fire.

Loki looked at him before turning his attention back to the pop and spit of the fire. "They call me L...Luke." Loki had to think quickly. He almost said his name was Loki but if Gareth knew what he was, he would definitely be suspicious of a god here in his cave.

"Well, Luke, it's going to be a long night. I have a bedroll I can set up here next to the fire for you. It should keep you warm enough through the night. You hungry, thirsty? Need anything before I go?"

"Go? Where are you going? You aren't going to leave me here, are you?"

Gareth chuckled, "You aren't afraid, are you? I thought you were an experienced hiker, after all."

"Well yeah, of course I am. I am just a little out of it after losing my pack and the pain from my leg and all."

"Gotcha. No, I am not leaving you for the night. I am just going to scout the area and make sure all is well. I want to get a feel for the weather and make sure the storm is going to hold off."

Loki nodded his head in understanding and watched his wayward rescuer disappear. As soon as he was sure he was out of sight, Loki flashed to Thor's side.

"What in the hell is going on? Is this a joke? You didn't tell me he was one of us," Loki choked out in anger.

"What are you talking about, Loki? One of us what? Who is?" Thor asked in confusion.

"Gareth is a half-god, he is one of us. He is half-troll and half-god. What if he can tell who I am? This is not funny," Loki gritted out.

"I swear I didn't know, she didn't tell me that part. Freyja is having a good old laugh at our expense, I can imagine. Relax, Loki, if he knew who you were, he would have said something I am sure. Plus he is no danger to you and you are in no danger from him, you can just leave without a second thought."

"Fine, but what the hell was that anyway? You really had to trip me and make me fall in front of him like that? I felt like a freaking idiot."

Thor's laughter filled the hall. "Relax, old friend, I need him to take care of you until the rescue crew shows up. They are so close to each other and they don't even know it. Just sit back and watch the fireworks."

Five

Gareth climbed up the mountain away from the cave and the stranger. "Mother, are you here? I could really use some help. I don't know what to do. Something is coming and I don't know if it's good or bad. Please, Mom, I need you." Gareth waited a few more minutes in vain, his mother hardly showed up when he called anymore.

He moved to lean against the rock face and stare out over the forest below. There wasn't any place like this in the world. Gareth could feel the stress and tension slowly easing away. It had been too long since he had time to get up here and commune with nature.

He knew that it was his troll blood that pulled at him to be away from the humans as much as he could, he wasn't cut out to be in such crowded places. His other half craved the excitement and comforts of living in town surrounded by people. He was constantly at war with himself; it was a never-ending battle that was slowly driving him insane.

Gareth stood with a sigh and headed back to the cave and his unfortunate guest. Something just didn't seem right about him, but he just couldn't place his finger on what it was. If only he was in tune with his god side a little more, maybe he could use it to his advantage.

Gareth stepped into the cave and took in the sight before him. Luke sat by the fire exactly where he had left him, with his head leaned back against the wall. A grimace flashed across his face; poor guy must be in pain.

"Are you okay? I don't have any pain meds to give you. I don't take anything like that or keep it on hand as I am not used to guests."

"It's quite all right. I can ignore the pain for the most part. Would you care to talk to help pass the time until nightfall comes?"

"I don't have much to say about myself, but I can tell you of some legends and myths that are associated with this area and the mountains if you care to listen."

"That would be much appreciated. Anything to keep my mind occupied would be greatly appreciated."

Gareth moved to sit against the opposite wall. "I don't know if you know it, but these mountains and well, this whole area is rife with tales of the Norse gods."

Loki/Luke perked up at that. "Really now? Norse gods in these parts? How did that come to be? Aren't they from the Germanic and Scandinavian countries mainly?"

Gareth chuckled at his enthusiasm. "That is correct. We have a large population of descendants here and they brought their gods with them, from what I was told."

"Well, do tell, I am quite curious to hear what you have to say of these noble gods."

Six

"This seems like a good place as any to make camp. We only have about an hour before we lose the light completely and I don't know about you guys, but I would rather be set up in comfort before then."

Jared and Quentin agreed and began readying the campsite. The brothers worked in companionable silence, each lost in their own heads.

"I am going to find some firewood if one of you want to prepare a spot," Zach called out as he headed off.

"I got it," said Jared. "Go ahead and finish what you are doing."

By the time Zach came back, the camp was set and a circle of stones had been set up. "You hungry?" Quentin asked as he tossed a bag of provisions at Zach before he could reply.

Zach grunted and sat down while Jared started the fire. When he was done, he laid back on the ground, looked up and watched the stars come out.

This was one of the best parts of being out here. You couldn't see the stars like this in town. Nothing could compare to the contentment he felt sitting here with his brothers and being with nature.

They didn't need to fill the silence, they were comfortable with it and each other in every way that mattered. Time passed and the night air cooled off enough to make them move closer to the fire.

Jared spoke softly into the night, "If you could break the curse, would you? I mean in all seriousness, would you? Knowing all the good things we can do because of it?"

Zach sighed and gathered his thoughts. "As much as I complain about it, and as hard as it makes dating, no, I don't think I could give it up. I just have to believe that one day I will find a guy out there who can handle all the baggage I come with."

"I wouldn't either," Quentin whispered. "Whenever I start to think like that, I just think of the faces of all the people we have saved, and I know that even though it was supposed to be a curse, it's not for those people. Even if they don't know about it."

"Do you guys really think we can find people to love us, human and goat?"

Quentin and Zach exchanged a look. Jared was the youngest of them and sometimes he took things harder. He was a lot like their mother in that aspect.

"I do, Jared, I really do. There has to be someone out there for all of us. The gods can't hate us that much." Zach rolled over and climbed to his feet. "I am going to call it a night, guys.

Let's be ready to head out as soon as the sky lightens enough to see."

"Where are we storing the extra gear?" Quentin called out.

"We can store it under the brush here, no one will find it. You have your special packs ready to go, right?"

Jared and Quentin acknowledged they did before they climbed to their feet and headed to bed as well.

Seven

Zach made sure each of his brothers' packs were securely on their backs before he too shifted into his goat form. One of the best things Quentin had ever done was design a bag that they could wear as they shifted that would hold the essentials they would need up on the mountain for whoever they found.

"You guys ready to go?" Zach asked them through their link. Both brothers nodded yes and Zach started climbing. He didn't know how long they would have before the storm hit and they needed to cover as much ground as they could before then.

"Why don't we split up a bit and look for any trace of a hiker being up here. Check in periodically so we all know where the others are and that we are okay," Zach projected to his brothers and watched as they both moved off in opposite directions.

In their human form they could climb faster than most people, in their animal form they were practically unstoppable.

The hours passed slowly and the promised storm sat on the horizon, constantly threatening but never landing. Zach hadn't found any trace of anyone being up here, but he wasn't ready to call it quits yet. He topped a small rise and stopped to take a breather.

"Are you guys as hungry as I am? Come join me for a lunch break and then we will regroup and continue our search."

Jared was the first to join. Always full of energy, he came bounding over, jumping and having a good time. Zach couldn't help but laugh at seeing him. It wasn't often you saw an almost 300 pound goat jump in joy. *"Settle down before you pull something, you freak."* Jared's laughter filled his head before it was replaced with Quentin's voice. *"Is he jumping again? There is just something wrong with a grown goat jumping like that."* Zach watched as Quentin joined them on the rise.

The three men shifted and threw some clothes on from their packs. "By the gods, it doesn't come with a better view anywhere I have ever seen," Jared said with reverence in his words. Zach paused in getting lunch out of his pack to look around. He was right, it never failed to amaze him how beautiful one place could be. He could bet that Valhalla would look something like this. Paradise in a word.

"Come on, guys, we are killing time. We can come back after we establish all is well. Have you guys seen any signs, smelled anything, heard anything?" Zach looked from brother to brother as they both shook their heads in the negative. "I am starting to think this is a wild goose chase. We are almost to the coordinates. After we eat, we can check up around that area and then decide what to do from there."

Jared nodded his agreement, still staring off into the distance. Zach turned to look at his youngest brother but he had moved off. He moved to follow him, but Quentin stopped him with his next words.

"He's okay, he just feels close to Dad whenever we are up here. Give him a few minutes and he will be back to normal."

Eight

Loki came awake slowly, forgetting for a minute where he was and the role he was playing. He stretched his sore muscles and turned to find his host watching him from the other side of the fire. "Is there a problem?" Loki said between yawns.

Gareth continued to stare for a few more seconds before looking back down to the fire. "No problem at all. I was just checking to make sure you were okay. You know, you were mumbling in your sleep. Something about killing Thor and hard ground."

Loki blushed, "Guess your stories resonated with me a bit more than I expected. What time is it anyway?"

Gareth turned to look out the cave entrance at the morning light. "I'd say probably a little after eight or so. The storm seems to be holding off for now, but I don't know how long that will last. We can try to head down the mountain and see how far we get before the storm hits, but then we have to hope we can find shelter, or we can sit tight and see what it does and make a decision later. It's up to you."

Loki pondered what to do. He couldn't really leave this cave otherwise how would the shifter find the troll?

He had to make this sound convincing though, Gareth was already suspicious of him. Damn gods blood! "I think we should stick around, I don't want to get caught out in that. I don't have my gear anymore and I don't think you have enough to sustain both of us out in that weather. Am I correct?"

"Yes, I have enough, but it would be tight. I can climb to higher ground and see if I can get a signal out. Your sat phone luckily was in your pocket when I found you. It doesn't seem to be broken." Gareth paused before continuing. "I don't have much, but if you are hungry you are welcome to share. I mean I have plenty, it's just not the most appetizing stuff you could have."

For the first time, Loki found a genuine grin crossing his face. "Bring on the hard tac and water. It's an adventure, right?"

Gareth supplied Loki with his breakfast, then cleaned up and headed out to see if he could get a signal. Chances were slim with the storm sitting off in the distance, but it wouldn't hurt to try. Plus, he wanted to see if he could get his mother again while he had the chance. Gareth climbed up to the top of the mountain and surveyed his surroundings. If he could live here forever, he would die a happy man. The air smelled cleaner and the cool breeze made him feel rejuvenated. He gave little thought to the man he left behind in the cave. He had left plenty of water and a blanket. The fire was built up and should last till he returned.

Gareth sat down on the ledge and took a deep breath, filling his lungs. It had taken him two hours to get up here and he wasn't rushing down for anything. After a few minutes, he pulled out the sat phone and checked the connection. Just what he expected, nothing, no signal. Damn storm!

"Mother, are you here?" he called out. Gareth was getting frustrated, it wasn't like his mother to not answer for this long of a stretch. Something kept nagging at the back of his mind that there were games afoot he wasn't aware of.

His biggest worry was the man in the cave. He had lied to him. He had plenty of food to get them off the mountain and back to civilization, but he wasn't sure he wanted him out of his cave yet. At least not until he knew why he felt some odd connection to him.

It's like his brain recognized him in some way, he just didn't know why he felt that way. Gareth had no doubt the stranger seeking refuge in his cave was lying to him. He just wasn't sure for what purpose.

Gareth spent the next couple hours just relaxing and taking in the beauty of the storm in the distance, the wind and the sun warming his body. He periodically called out to his mother, with no more success. Each failed attempt left him more annoyed than the last.

As the sun slowly descended through the skies to its resting place, Gareth stood and started his climb back to the cave. He had waited too long and now he would have to rush back to make it before dark fell and his guest became worried about his ability to traverse these mountains in the dark.

Nine

Zach was sure they were wasting their time now. This was the spot and there was no sign of anyone having been here. No body, no blood, no equipment. Nothing. *"You guys find anything?"*

"Nada," Jared said in a resigned tone. Zach waited but heard nothing from Quentin. *"Quentin, you okay, bro?"* Zach was getting impatient and nervous about his lack of response.

"I'm here, sorry. There is a cave up here and I smelled smoke. I was going to check it out, but I think you guys need to get up here and see for yourselves."

"I'm close to the cave, I will be there in a hop, skip and a jump. Okay, well maybe just in a jump or two," Jared called out with laughter tinting his every word.

Zach groaned at his brother's antics, he knew Jared walked a fine line between irritating Quentin and pissing him off till he retaliated.

"I'm below that a bit, it will take me a few minutes to get up there, I have to go around a couple big rocks. Be careful and I'll see you in a minute. Oh, and Quentin, don't kill him, please."

"No guarantees he won't accidentally fall...off the side of the mountain...or just fall down in general." Zach rolled his eyes and didn't even bother replying. There wasn't any point.

He reversed his path on the trail he was on to start his climb up to the cave. It would be his luck to have to backtrack to get past this point. He was anxious to get up there and see what had caused such an odd reaction to the cave and some smoke.

Would that mean they had found their lost hiker? Why else would there be smoke in a cave? He hoped the hiker was okay, it was going to be difficult getting him down this mountain if he was hurt. The gods knew nothing was ever easy for them, plus add in that damnable storm sitting there taunting them and he knew they were in for a trip from hell. No way could a rescue helicopter get close with that storm.

***

Loki turned to watch the cave entrance, he could feel the brothers watching and waiting. He was bored and they could provide some much needed entertainment. "Hey, boys, I know you are there. Come join me." Luke smiled as he detected no movement from them. Time to take matters into his own hands. He stood up and headed to the cave entrance.

"Don't just hide there like scared little goats hiding from the big bad troll. Come in and enjoy the fire. I swear to you on all that I hold dearly, you are safe here." Loki paused and waited. "Seriously, for the gods' sake, I know you are there. It's pointless to keep hiding.

Loki smiled as the two men stood and moved to entrance. "See, that wasn't so bad, was it? Wait, where is the third brother? And what is your name, gorgeous?" Loki licked his lips as he looked Quentin up and down.

"Who are you? How do you know who we are?" Quentin asked with suspicion lacing his every word. He couldn't explain the odd tingle that ran down his spine as he looked into the stranger's eyes.

"Calm down, goat boy. I was sent down here to help an old friend. And to your question, I know more than who you are, I know about your curse, who put it on you and what you have done with it."

"Spectacular, by the way, I applaud you for that noble gesture, even if the stupid humans are clueless as to how you manage these miraculous saves." Loki turned and headed back into the cave. "Come, we have much to discuss before the fireworks start in a few minutes. We will want a good seat, I promise you."

The brother's exchanged a look of confusion before following Loki in the cave.

"Sit with your backs to the wall with me. This way we can see when they enter and their reactions. Yes, I will explain while we wait." Loki rolled his eyes as he sat back down and waited for the brothers to do the same. "Come on, sit next to me. I promise I will keep my hands to myself...for now." Loki winked at Quentin and turned his attention to the ground around him, making sure he had left just enough room that he would have to sit close.

Loki looked up to them and rolled his eyes, "I promise to behave. Besides, if I was going to hurt you there wouldn't be anything you could do to stop me. I am a god, after all."

The brothers both backed up a step, wariness evident on their shocked faces. "I told you I mean you no harm. I'm here to help an old friend make up for what he did to your family."

"Thor," Quentin growled out in anger. Jared sucked in a breath and narrowed his eyes at Loki.

"Who in the hell are you?" Jared spit out between clenched jaws.

"Loki, at your service," he said with a charming smile and a devilish gleam in his eyes. "In more ways than one, if you want."

Quentin rolled his eyes, "The trickster god, that so makes me want to trust you now. Why did he send you and what does he want after all these years? He cursed us and then left us to fend for ourselves."

Loki chewed on his bottom lip and contemplated the two brothers standing before him. He needed Thor to get his hairy ass down here and explain this shit. "I promise Thor will explain shortly, or I will kick his eternal ass. For now, just sit and wait. Things will make sense shortly."

The brothers still didn't trust Loki and he didn't blame them. For once, though, he wasn't screwing around. "Tell me something, if you don't mind."

Quentin settled down against the wall and turned to face him. "What?"

"Why were you sitting out there staring in here? What made you hesitant to come in?"

"I could sense something was off in here, I assume it was your powers I felt. It wasn't just that though. There is a smell in here that made me wary. I don't know why, but I felt it in my bones." Quentin shrugged as if that would explain it all.

"You might have felt my powers, but it's more than that. It's a troll," Loki said with a shake of his head in acknowledgment.

The two brothers shared a look of confusion before turning back to Loki and waiting for an explanation.

"Troll, that's what you smelled, or in this case a half-troll. Don't worry, he means you no harm either. He has been nothing but hospitable since I...um, never mind about that. Trust me," Loki said with a wink. "You are perfectly safe here."

Quentin groaned, "I bet he was hospitable." He growled out in anger, he wasn't quite sure why that thought pissed him off so much but it did. Then another thought came to him. "Wait, you bastard! You are the missing hiker, aren't you?"

Jared cocked his head in puzzlement and frowned at his brother, "Why do you think that?"

"We can get back to that in a minute. Your brother and the troll are approaching. Fireworks are about to explode." Loki grinned and almost vibrated with excitement.

Ten

Gareth slowed as he neared the cave, something was off. He moved closer to the entrance and peered in to see three men leaning against the wall. "Luke, everything okay?" he called out as he approached the wall where they sat watching him.

"No worries, Gareth. All is well…finally," he muttered the last word under his breath, almost too quietly for him to hear.

"Who are you two and what is that amazing smell?" Gareth asked in puzzlement as he looked at the two brothers.

"These are the Maddux brothers," Loki said with a purr as he glanced at Quentin again. "They are part of search and rescue and my guess is they are here on the mountain looking for me, the missing hiker."

Gareth frowned and tried to figure out what he was missing, he couldn't concentrate though. That smell was driving him crazy. He had never felt like this in his life. His blood was raging, and his stomach was doing somersaults. He felt like something he had been unconsciously missing was finally within his grasp.

***

Zach was getting worried again. It had taken far longer than he expected to make it to the cave and his brothers weren't answering his calls. He stopped and shifted into his human form and quickly dressed. Zach hesitated as he neared the entrance where he could sense his brothers were waiting.

He stopped suddenly in his steps, almost like he hit a wall. He closed his eyes and waited for the jittery feeling going down his spine to settle so he could walk again.

The cave was calling him in. No, not the cave, something or someone inside was. It was a pull in the center of his chest. With slow, cautious steps he entered the cave and froze as he met the eyes of the man standing a few feet away. His jaw dropped and he struggled to take a deep breath in. Zach licked his lips and waited for the man to say something. He knew he couldn't, he was stunned speechless. Hell, he didn't want to ever stop staring at him.

"Who are you?" Gareth asked in a whisper full of awe and longing.

"Zach. Who are you?" Zach said in a raspy, lust-filled voice.

"Gareth, and by the gods, you smell amazing." Gareth cringed as he said those words. Now he sounded like a psychopath.

Zach grinned, "I was going to say the same about you."

"On that note, I think it's time you get down here, big guy, before these two go from eye fucking to just fucking in front of us. On second thought, take your time. That could be hot as hell," Loki called out as he looked up to the ceiling of the cave.

"No, no, it's not hot. That's my brother, you asshat," Jared shouted in disgust.

Loki grunted in disappointment and rolled his eyes, "Fine, it's time. Get down here and fill them in, please."

"Luke, who are you talking to?" Gareth asked in bewilderment.

"Luke? That seems so normal a name for you," Quentin ground out as he stood to his feet and moved to Zach's side. "Zach, meet the god Loki. Who, if I am not mistaken, is also our missing hiker?"

"God?" Zach and Gareth said at the same time.

"Yes, yes, that's me." Loki stood with a flourish and bowed to them. "If you will excuse me one moment, I have to fetch someone." Loki smiled at Quentin, "Don't go anywhere, handsome, I am so coming back for you."

"What in the hell is going on here?" Zach demanded as he turned to Gareth.

"I have no idea. All I know is that man claimed his name was Luke. I stumbled upon him on the trail and he fell and hurt his leg.

I knew something wasn't right with him. I could sense it, but didn't know what it was. I now know it was his god powers I was sensing. I'm not that in tune with that half of my DNA."

Before anyone could respond, Loki flashed back into the cave with another man. "Gareth, Zach, other brother and gorgeous brother which I really need to learn your name, meet Thor."

Gareth had to grab Zach as he rushed forward with a bellow of anger at his words. "Why are you here? Haven't you done enough to my family? What more do you want from us?" Zach growled out between clenched teeth.

Thor raised one eyebrow and glanced at Loki. "Feisty, isn't he. You think Gareth is up to the challenge?"

Zach cursed at his words and turned to the man holding him. "Get your hands off me, now."

Gareth sighed in disappointment and stepped back, glaring holes at the two gods. He wasn't sure what was going on, but he knew it was their doing.

"What a shame, I was enjoying that a little too much I think," Loki said with a wicked smile. He turned and looked to Quentin. "So, sexy, can I get your name? I want to know whose name I will be calling out in bed after all."

Quentin sputtered in shock before finally finding his voice. "It won't be mine. I don't want anything to do with the gods and their fickle ways."

Zach was furious at Loki's words. "Leave my family alone. You gods have done nothing but hurt us. What did we do now that you have come back into our lives?"

Thor stepped forward, "You've got it wrong, I came to make restoration to your family. I can't in good conscious take away your abilities, you have given so much to the mortals around here."

Zach laughed in disbelief, the high shrill sound clearly mocking the god's words. "When has a god ever given two shits about a mortal? We are barely a blip on your radar. Our lives are snuffed out in the blink of an eye to you."

Loki shrugged in agreement with that statement. He couldn't deny Zach's words. Thor frowned, "Loki, you ass, you aren't supposed to agree with him. You are on my side, remember?"

"You are my friend but damn, look at his brother. I will do anything to get on his good side." Loki growled and licked his lips. "He is just so yummy."

Thor rolled his eyes at his longtime friend and turned his attention back to Zach. "Forget him. I am here to help you, no ulterior motives. I know I cursed your family long ago, to be honest a lot longer than I realized.

I started watching you and came to the realization that you took my curse and turned it into something amazing. I can't take it away, but I can help you find happiness."

Jared smiled a cocky smile and chimed in, "Who says we aren't happy?"

"Oh my poor, delusional boy, don't you know you can't lie to gods? We see everything. I know you aren't." Thor smiled placatingly.

"Why are you here in my cave then? I haven't been cursed by any of you." Gareth looked around at all the people who had invaded his sanctuary.

"That's just it, Gareth. You are going to end up being what makes him happy," he said as he pointed to Zach. "You are his mate, his other half."

Gareth eyes widened in surprise, "That is the connection I feel then. The overwhelming urge to just be near him, to look at him."

Loki smiled, "If he were my mate, I think I would have the urge to do a lot more than that."

Zach frowned, "You gods are all alike, do what you want and fuck everyone else. I want nothing to do with it or any of you." With one last glance at Gareth, Zach turned his back and headed back out of the cave.

"Oh and by the way, Loki, you better get back to where the search and rescue team is looking for you. Don't make them search for nothing and chance getting hurt because you gods decided to interfere once again."

Eleven

Gareth watched as the other half of his soul walked out of his cave, trailed by his brothers. He fell to his knees as pain ripped through him. He clutched his chest and cried out in agony. "What is happening?" He looked desperately to the gods for answers but they shook their heads with a look of bewilderment on their faces.

"I know not, I have never seen this before," Thor said in a shocked voice as he slowly approached and laid a hand on Gareth's shoulder.

His touch slowly eased the pain raging through his aching body and finally Gareth could take a deep breath again. "What did you do?" He looked to Thor for answers that were not coming.

"I did nothing, it would seem your soul is crying out in pain because your other half rejected you. I am sorry, there is nothing I can do to repair this. Until you two are bonded, the pain will continue to grow and eventually kill you." Thor smiled sympathetically, "I will help you. This is my fault."

Loki frowned in puzzlement, "How come I have never heard of this before? Is it because he is part god or part troll? Or maybe just because he is mated to a shifter?"

"No, it's because they both recognized their connection, their souls connected and have now been torn apart."

"Zach is going through the same pain then?" Gareth whispered

"I'm not sure to be honest. I have temporarily blocked your pain. It's a stopgap at most. It isn't permanent. The more time that passes, the weaker the block will become." Thor stopped and glanced to Loki. "Go be found by the rescue team, I will meet you at home after I speak to Freyja and see if she will assist or at least provide some insight into these matters."

Loki nodded and left the cave. Gareth looked to Thor. "So what do I do, continue on as nothing has happened? You brought him into my life and then let him walk away. You are slowly killing me and you are going to just leave. Maybe my mother was right when she told me to avoid the gods."

"No, my boy. I will figure this out, I will be back soon with a plan. I will get you together if it's the last thing I do."

"No offense, but I don't think I want your help. He hates the gods and it would seem understandably so. I have to convince him to give me a chance without you making it worse. He knows I am half-god now, too. The odds are against me." With that Gareth stood, grabbed his pack and left the cave to head back to his home in town.

***

Zach fumed silently the whole way back down the mountainside. Their trek was slow due to the darkness that slowly descended upon them. His anger was too great to allow him to stop and rest for the night. He wanted off this mountain and as far away from the gods and their games as he could get.

"Are we just going to walk out on him? He is your mate, your other half. How can you leave him?" Jared called out to Zach through their connection.

Zach didn't respond, just kept climbing down. There was nothing he could say that would make Jared understand. He was torn in two.

He wanted to know more about Gareth, to spend the rest of his days discovering everything he could about the gorgeous man, but he was part god. He wasn't sure he could handle that; gods were devious, underhanded, and arrogant assholes at the best of times.

"I understand what is going through you head, brother. Just don't let your hate for his parent hold you from what you can have with him. He may not be like them." Quentin tried to get through to his brother, but Zach had blocked all communication from them.

The hours passed and they slowly made their way to the bottom and shifted back to human form. They donned their clothes and packs and continued on their way.

By morning, they had made it back to the rescue site headquarters and were greeted by their old friend.

"Morning, boys, didn't quite expect to see you for a few hours yet." Mack grinned and patted them on their backs. "Good news, the hiker was found and accounted for. The rescue team is on their way back with the hiker in tow."

Zach released a breath he hadn't been aware he was holding. "Everyone's okay, no problems?" If any of the rescue team had gotten hurt because of Loki and Thor's games, he would make them pay.

"Yeah, no problems at all. They reported no issues, said it was a smooth hike. They should be here within the next two hours."

Zach exchanged looks with his brothers and nodded. "I'm glad you found him. If you don't mind, we are going to head out."

"Of course, sorry we called you out on a wild goose chase," Mack said with a smile as he turned and headed back to the trailer they used as base of operations.

The brothers loaded their gear and silently headed back to their home at camp headquarters.

***

Thor paced back and forth, lost in thought as Loki lounged behind him on a cushioned chaise, lost in thought if the smile on his face was any indication.

"What has gotten into you two?" Sif demanded as she entered the room. "You look like a love sick pup, Loki, and you, my darling husband, look way too contemplative. What is going on?"

Thor growled in frustration, "Damn Freyja won't answer me and I can't find her. The oldest brother, Zach, took one look at our halfling and connected. As soon as he found out we were involved he took off, leaving Gareth's soul to splinter."

Sif frowned, "What happened to his soul? Is that even possible?"

Loki, still lost in his thoughts, didn't even look up. Thor sighed and shrugged, "I had never heard of it myself, but when I laid my hand on his shoulder I felt it. I caused this and I have to fix it."

"Well, then let's see what we can do to resolve this little problem of yours. Though it should be said this is what you get for interfering in the lives of mortals." Sif looked down on the Isle of Man and watched.

Thor shook his head and resumed his pacing, every once in a while throwing Loki a glare. The imbecile had been useless since he returned from his venture in the caves.

"The brothers run a camp for kids. They are having a benefit to raise money. I think that is a perfect place to bring the two halves back together." Thor looked up excitedly at his wife's words.

"Brilliant idea. Do you hear that, Loki? We have a party to crash." Loki didn't acknowledge his words once again.

"What is the matter with him?" Sif asked, bewildered.

"I have no earthly idea. He has been like that since we returned. In all these centuries, I have never seen him like this. It's almost like he is love-struck. The idea makes me shudder at the prospect." Thor's quiet words made Sif's curiosity peak.

"In the meantime, you have two weeks to figure out how to get Gareth there. Think you can handle that? I have something I need to check on." Sif kissed her husband's cheek and strolled off to find Freyja and see if her suspicions were correct.

Twelve

Gareth paced the small confines of his apartment feeling even more penned in than usual. A week had passed and he was slowly going mad. The pain was coming and going but nothing like that first few minutes. He knew his time was ticking away. His body burned for the touch of Zach, but he didn't know how to repair what the gods had done. Hell, he didn't even know how to find his partner. Gareth frowned as a shred of memory came back to him, he had been so caught up in the sight, smell and feel of having his other half that close, he had barely paid attention. He remembered Loki saying something about meeting the brothers. He paced faster and racked his brain, trying to recall the name he had used.

"Maddux, that was it. Zach Maddux." It was official, he had lost what little mind he had. He was talking to himself now. Damn the gods, this was another thing he blamed on them.

Gareth threw himself down on the threadbare couch and grabbed his laptop to do some digging. It was time to do something besides pace and curse at the gods for their helping hand.

***

Zach was fighting it with everything he had. He barely knew Gareth but that didn't matter to his mind, body or soul. They had claimed him and that was the end of it.

"Zach, you okay? The planners are here to go over last minute details about the benefit this weekend." Quentin eyed him up and down, worry etching on his face.

"What benefit?" Zach questioned.

Quentin rolled his eyes and let out a sigh, things were worse than he had realized. "The benefit we have been planning for two months, the one to bring in the money to continue operating for those kids. You remember our camp, right?"

"Of course I remember, you jackass. I just temporarily forgot it was this weekend." Zach glanced around his desk and sheepishly shrugged, "What day is it anyway?"

"For fuck's sake, seriously?" Quentin couldn't believe he had heard him right. Zach was so lost, he had let everything else just disappear. Hell, Quentin was struggling himself, but he was still able to function. Why couldn't Zach? "It's Wednesday, the benefit is Saturday night."

"Never mind, I'll have Jared help me make the last minute plans. That means you have to deal with the phone though. We have a new home calling wanting to set up a retreat for their kids. Think you can handle that?" Quentin snarled as he stormed out of the room.

Zach sat their stunned at his brother's odd behavior. He had been a little out of sorts, he admitted that, but that attitude hadn't been warranted. He picked up the phone to make the arrangements and made a mental note to track Jared down as soon as he was done to see what he knew of Quentin's odd behavior.

Half an hour later and Zach was exhausted mentally. What should have been a routine scheduling of a camp out had become a battle. The stubborn woman wouldn't cooperate and provide names of the staff. She had some bullshit excuse as to why, but it didn't make sense to him.

He had never had a home refuse before. It wasn't that big a deal, it was just a formality to help when the campers arrived. They would have lists of campers and counselors assigned to cabins. Now they would have to add counselor names the day of.

Jared strolled in fuming. "I can't take you two asshats anymore. Something has to be done," he seethed between clenched jaws.

"What are you rambling on about? I haven't done anything to you," Zach grumbled out as he stood and grabbed his pacing brother so he could talk to him face to face.

"You haven't done anything is the point. You have been so preoccupied with not seeing your soulmate that you have become a recluse in this office. You hardly ever leave, or eat or shower.

I can't do this on my own and I shouldn't have to." Jared wrenched himself free of Zach's hands and continued on pacing. "Quentin isn't much better, you know. He makes a show of attempting to work, but his head is somewhere else, too. I don't know what is going on but between the two of you, I am going to quit and go shack up somewhere away from you both until you get this shit out of your system."

Zach didn't have a chance to utter a single word before Jared was gone with a slam of the office door. He wasn't sure how long he stood there staring before he became aware of the pain building again.

"Not now," he mumbled as he slowly sank to his knees, trying to manage the pain that wracked his exhausted body. The pains were happening more and more frequently and he didn't know why. The doctor had done a full work up and everything had come back with his meaningless stamp of approval. Zach wasn't sure where he had found his license but there was definitely something wrong with him, no matter what the quack doctor had said.

"Zach, the bene…" Quentin trailed off as he saw Zach on the floor. "Not again, there has to be something we can do. Jared, help. Zach's down again," Quentin bellowed for his brother as he attempted to lift Zach from the floor and onto the couch.

Jared came running in and together they assisted the groaning man to lie down. "We have to figure this out, it started after the cave and you know who. Maybe the gods did something to him."

"What do you want us to do, just call out and say, 'Hey gods. We need some answers. Loki, Thor, any of you listening?'"

"You don't…" Jared's words were cut off as Loki appeared behind them.

"Hello, hotstuff, I was hoping you would call me sooner rather than later."

Quentin jerked around in surprise at Loki's words. "Fuck me, what are you doing here?"

"Oh, an invitation I will happily accept, just lead the way, stud muffin. I promise to make you scream out my name," Loki purred as he stepped closer to Quentin. "Just don't call out to any god in general, I don't need to kill any of them tonight."

Quentin looked frantically left and right but he was trapped between the muscular body of Loki and the couch his brother was reclining on.

"That blush is sexy, I didn't expect that. Wonder what else turns red with attention." Loki dipped his eyes down Quentin's body, assessing him.

"Excuse me, Loki, but since you are here, can you stop ogling my brother for a minute and help us out?" Jared pushed his way between the two men and pointed to Zach.

Loki rolled his eyes, "Damn, boy, you just ruined the best thing I had going tonight." He looked over Jared's shoulder and met Quentin's eyes. "Later, baby. I will keep my promise, don't you worry." Loki turned and took Zach in. "Well, what's wrong? I'm not a mind reader and while you are at it, tell me why you called me for your sick brother anyway."

Jared rolled his eyes and mumbled about horny gods and their lack of thinking abilities. "He has been having these attacks since we left your asses at the cave. What did you gods do to him?"

"Oh, that. We didn't do it to them. They did that all on their own. Stubborn idiots denying what is in front of them. They connected, their souls bonded. You can't just separate that shit. It will kill you, as you can see."

Jared and Quentin's eyes bugged at the gods lackadaisical words. "What? Oh shit. Sorry, Sif is always yelling at me about that. I don't think before I speak," Loki said with a shrug of one shoulder. "He needs to accept Gareth as his other half, and do it fast before they both die."

"Shit, do you have to talk like that in front of him?" Quentin growled in frustration and anger at the news.

"Calm down, sex on a stick. He passed out from the pain and I would guess stress." Loki moved to go around Jared to get back to Quentin's side.

"Excuse me, I have to go," Quentin said as he scurried out of the room and away from the lustful eyes of the god.

"I hate to see him go, but what a view as he leaves." Loki tsked in appreciation before turning back to the gaping baby brother. "What, he is seriously hot."

Jared rolled his eyes and turned back to Zach. "So basically we need to get him and Gareth together."

"Basically, yeah. Thor and I have a plan about that actually. The benefit you boys are putting on would be a great starting point. Now that we have your aide, it will be much easier to convince your brother to do what we need without him knowing us despised gods are involved." Loki frowned and chewed his lip before hesitantly asking his next question. "Do all of you hate us gods?"

Jared was shocked by his question, that was the last thing he had expected and definitely in not such a meek and shy tone of voice. "We don't trust you, and at different points in our lives we have hated you for what was cursed upon us, but no, we don't hate you in general."

Loki beamed at Jared's words. "Then I have a chance. Good to know. Now back to the benefit. Thor is going to handle getting Gareth there, you just have to make sure your brother is in the right place at the right time."

"How the hell am I supposed to know when the time and place is?"

"Patience, my boy, all in good time. I promise you will know all you need before the party this weekend. Until then, tell your luscious brother I will be dreaming of him and I will talk to you later."

Loki disappeared as quick as he had come and left Jared with more questions than answers.

He glanced to his still passed out brother and smiled. This was going to be fun, he missed his lighthearted brother from years before. Zach had changed in many ways after the man he thought was his future walked away and laughed at their curse. The bastard had even tried to have Zach committed to a psych ward. Zach needed a happy ending with a man who could love him as a man and as a goat.

"Why are you staring at me like I grew another head?" Zach groused out as he pulled himself to a sitting position on the couch. "The bastard god didn't curse me again, did he?" Zach questioned half-jokingly.

"Sorry, no, nothing like that. I was just lost in my thoughts. That must have been a bad attack, you actually passed out from it this time." Jared's eyes wandered the room searching for something to distract his brother.

"Did you ever tell me what happened with the planners? Is the event all set or did Quentin scare them off with his surly attitude?"

"No, it wasn't that. He just wasn't paying attention and then would randomly ask a question that had already been discussed or throw out an idea for something that was totally irrelevant. It was embarrassing. Everyone could tell he wasn't paying attention is all. Things are all set though. Planners are ready to go and I think we have nothing to worry about, it will go off without a hitch."

"Are you okay? You seem nervous and you're rambling. You only do that when you are hiding something or feel guilty."

"I just...um...feel bad that I was getting mad at you for not helping, but you are dealing with these attacks of pain like that." Jared smiled weakly and backed toward the door. "I'm gonna go check out Quentin and let him know you are awake and okay."

Zach wasn't sure what that was all about, but he could sense a lie when he heard one. Jared was keeping something from him. He could only hope he knew what he was doing and wasn't screwing with anything that would hurt them.

Thirteen

When Gareth had come home and found the invitation stuck to his door, he had been excited and jubilant with the knowledge his mate wanted him there. It wasn't long before reality sank in; Zach didn't know where he lived or even Gareth's last name. He had angrily stalked into his apartment and dropped onto the couch with an aggravated sigh of disappointment.

"Why are you so depressed?" Thor's disembodied voice floated to him from his kitchen before the large god appeared with a bottle of beer in hand. "Hope you don't mind. I love beer and since I was waiting for you to show up I had a peak around your dwelling. Kinda empty and desolate, isn't it?"

Gareth shrugged as he looked around the sparsely furnished room and saw it from his perspective. "Perhaps it is, but no one visits and I am rarely here myself. It suits my needs and that is what counts. Now, care to tell me why you are here in my house in the first place?

"Consider me your fairy godfather, here to grant your fondest wish, of course." Thor chuckled at Gareth's eye roll. "Okay, fine, I won't go that far, but I am here to help you get what you desire."

"And just what is that?"

"Zach, of course." Thor beamed in satisfaction with his own answer. "That invitation is to their benefit tonight. You will be attending, no ifs, ands, or buts about it."

"Impossible, that man made it clear he didn't want anything to do with me when he stormed out of the cave without so much as a look at me. He forgot I existed the minute you showed up."

"He can't forget you, there is nothing is his life that means as much to him as you. Okay, well besides his brothers, and rescuing lost hikers, and his camp for disadvantaged kids. But you are still tied at the top of those with his brothers. Oh, never mind. The important thing is he needs you, craves you, dreams of you and is dying without you. Just as you are without him."

"Am I to assume that the great god Thor's plan is to play matchmaker by having me attend the brothers' benefit? Isn't that a bit cliché?"

Thor rolled his eyes "What do you take me for, a meddling house wife? Of course that isn't it. That is only the beginning. Just be there tonight and trust me." Thor set his empty bottle on the coffee table and stood, "Wear the suit I left hanging in your closet. Oh, and how is the pain?"

"It's been bearable since you did your voodoo shit. It comes and goes and is happening more often, but it's tolerable and even with its current frequency, it only happens a couple times a week."

Thor nodded and smiled. "Good, then we aren't in danger yet. Have fun tonight and remember to trust me."

Gareth snorted at Thor's words. Who in their right mind would trust a god to have their best interest at heart?

***

Thor was excited. If all went well tonight, the first of the brothers would have his happily ever after. Things were going as planned and with a little luck, tonight would be a rousing success and he could relieve himself of some of the uncharacteristic guilt he carried over leaving the curse in place so long.

"Good news, my friend. Things are all set. I spoke to Freyr and he has agreed to play his part and will be at the benefit ready and willing to assist us in this matter. He was delighted to help, something about meddling in the affairs of mortals or some such nonsense," Loki called out as he met Thor in the center of the room.

"This is great news, I just left Gareth. He balked but I don't see him wasting an opportunity to be near Zach. The poor boys don't have a clue what is coming. This is going to be fun, maybe we should do this more often. It would be a great way to relieve our boredom."

"You've gone daft, haven't you? What are we, some meddlesome women to play matchmaker? Wake up, we are gods." Loki waited and then burst into laughter. "Sorry, I couldn't say that with a straight face. Playing in the affairs of mortals has always been a favorite past time, but I had never honestly thought of doing it in this way. I think it's something we should definitely look into."

Thor grinned at his old friend. "It's time. Let the fun begin."

***

Zach cursed as he once again fiddled with the tie around his neck. He felt like he was suffocating. The cloying smell of the benefit attendees' perfume and cologne was playing havoc on his heightened shifter nose.

He searched the crowded room and scowled, he would have sworn he felt Gareth's presence a moment ago. No matter how hard he tried, he couldn't find him in the crowd and it was driving him insane.

"It's almost time for the speech. Are you coming on stage with us or are you going to sit here and pout?" Jared asked from behind Zach's back.

"I'm not pouting, you overgrown sheep. I was getting a feel for the room and its occupants, that's all."

"My bad, it looked to me like you were searching for someone. Maybe a certain half-troll we all know and you love?"

Zach growled in warning before turning to face his youngest brother. "Where is Quentin to come save you before I kick your hairy ass?"

Jared grinned and nodded his head in the direction of the stage. "Sitting over there staring into his drink and lost in thought as usual. Sure don't know what's up with you guys, but I hope something happens soon. This is getting old." Jared winked and sidestepped around Zach before he could do something to embarrass them in front of their guests. "It's time, are you going to join us on stage?"

Zach nodded and followed with a permanent scowl etched into his features.

***

Gareth slid through the crowd as smoothly as he could, avoiding Zach and his searching eyes as he was instructed to by Thor. He didn't know what the gods had planned but he was willing to give them the benefit of the doubt.

Zach was close, he could feel him, it was as if his very molecules were connected to his. He felt this overwhelming urge to go to his soul.

Gareth checked his watch and sighed, gods be damned, if something didn't happen soon he was going to go insane from being so close to him.

"Ladies and gentleman, our hosts would like to thank you for coming tonight, but before I turn the mic over to them..." Gareth tuned the speaker out and searched for a spot to stand where he could see without being seen from the brothers standing on the stage.

Gareth leaned against the wall and searched the stage. Where was Zach, why wasn't he up there like he was supposed to be? He could feel his presence so he knew he was close, but he couldn't see him. The speaker took a step to the left and suddenly it was like the room lit up. Gareth couldn't contain the excitement that was roaring through his veins.

His blood was dancing a jig and burning him alive from the inside. Delicious heat poured through his entire body. Gareth stared at Zach and even though he knew he wasn't supposed to, he prayed for Zach to turn and meet his eyes. He needed to see him, to know that he was close by. For the first time in days his pain was forgotten, the ache nothing more than a fleeting memory in the face of seeing his other half so close.

"It's almost time, my boy. Just stay strong and you can have your man. I promise." Thor's quiet words filtered in through the noise of the crowd, breaking Gareth's concentration. He looked around, puzzled, but couldn't find the god.

"No worries, we wouldn't leave you at a time like this. Well, I might if that delicious piece of grade A prime beef would just give me a chance." Gareth rolled his eyes at Loki's words. You would think he was a God of lust or playboys or some such sex maniac type.

"Loki, can you please concentrate for one minute? How are we supposed to do this matchmaking thing if you can't pay attention and stop ogling people?"

Gareth choked on his laughter, had he just heard them right? A matchmaking service run by the gods Loki and Thor. "Did you just say matchmaking service? What would two old gods know about that?"

Thor scoffed at the note of laughter in Gareth's voice, "I think we are doing amazingly well for you, Gareth."

"Right, like the part where I am dying and am in pain from my mate rejecting me? Or maybe the part where I'm here at a benefit while my soul is standing across the room and I am waiting on gods, one of who can't think of anything but sex. Yeah, real inspiring work so far there, big guy."

"Pardon me, but I only lust after that one man. Though if I was honest, man isn't the right term for him. He is an Adonis, perfection incarnate."

"For the gods' sake, Loki, pay attention and help me here. And as to you, Gareth, it's not smart to mock gods, we are known to spite people. Your mate's family for instance."

"Of course, spite me. That would go over fantastic to potential clients in the future. I can hear it now. 'Yes, we have matched couples before.' ... 'Well, only one couple so far has been attempted.' ... 'Yes, I said attempted.' ... 'I spited the fool for mocking me.' ... 'Wait, where are you going? I'm fired? You can't fire a god.' Yeah, your brilliance in spiting me, Thor, would do wonders for your business."

"You are such a cheeky bastard," Thor growled out as he tried to hide his laughter.

Fourteen

Thor surveyed the crowded room and delighted in what he saw. Everything was set according to plan. Things couldn't have gone any smoother if he had tried. He spied the god Freyr and smiled. Let the show begin.

"Welcome, my friend, has Gareth been pointed out to you?" Thor asked expectantly as he continued to scan the room.

"Yes, he is quite handsome. This is one task I relish in undertaking." Freyr licked his lips as he surveyed the people around him. "So many mortals and so little time."

"Keep it in your pants until after you set the plan in motion. And just remember, Gareth and Zach are off limits. Your only objective is to make Zach notice you and Gareth. We need him to come to his senses and be with his mate."

Freyr rolled his eyes and spoke with boredom ringing in every word, "Yes, yes, I know. Your sidekick explained it to me already."

***

Zach climbed the short steps to the stage and stopped next to his brothers. He eagerly scanned the crowd in search of Gareth. He was here, he could feel him, he just couldn't see him.

Jared elbowed him in the side, "Dude, stop scowling and smile, people are watching and we need them to donate."

He vaguely heard his brother talking, but his attention was focused on the scene on the other side of the hall.

There stood Gareth talking to another man. Zach couldn't help his scowl as he watched the stranger smile and squeeze his mate's arm. He could feel his anger building deep inside. If this speaker didn't shut up soon so he could get off the stage, he was going to leave and say fuck it. No one was going to touch his mate in front of him.

Zach couldn't stop staring as the stranger flirted and continued touching his mate. What in the hell was Gareth thinking allowing this piece of shit to touch him like that? He didn't belong to the stranger and he damn well knew it.

"Excuse me, I have to go," Zach whispered to his brother as he jumped from the stage and headed to put an end to the budding relationship in front of him.

The crowd applauded and surged forward as if in a stampede to get to the front of the room first. Zach huffed and elbowed his way through the throng of people who were moving in his path as if they were unconsciously creating a barricade.

***

Gareth groaned as the stranger leaned forward and whispered in his ear yet again. The persistent ass wouldn't get the message he wasn't interested. How else could he say it before the idiot got the point?

"I'm sorry, maybe you misunderstood, but I am not interested. I am sure someone here would love your attention, but it isn't me."

"Why would I want someone else when the most gorgeous man in the room is standing in front of me?" Freyr winked and licked his lips, trying to entice Gareth.

"Like I have said multiple times, no, now please, for the love of the Gods, go away."

"Have a drink with me first."

"Fine, whatever, just go away." Gareth really wasn't sure what he had just said. All his attention was on the man pushing his way through the crowd toward him.

"Hello again," Gareth said tentatively as Zach came to a stop before him. Gods, the man looked amazing.

"What are you doing here?" Zach growled and narrowed his eyes, "Forget I asked that, the more important question is what are you doing allowing that overgrown ape to hang on you like that?"

Gareth's temper skyrocketed at his words. Let him? Did he really say that? What right did Zach have to throw a hissy fit over some man paying him attention? "What does it matter to you? You don't want me, you left me standing in that cave and didn't even look back. Now you can't handle someone else paying me any attention? Make up your mind, you can't have it both ways."

Zach growled again and stepped closer so they were touching from chest to thighs. "You can't deny we belong together, so why are you allowing him to touch you?"

"We may but you don't care, why should I?" Gareth narrowed his eyes, "Maybe he can put out the fire you started and then walked away from." A slow evil smile quirked his face, "As a matter of fact, I think there is an empty private bathroom just down the hall. Let's see if he can indeed fill...my needs."

Gareth turned and headed off to find the good-looking stranger that a short time ago had annoyed the living shit out of him. Before he could take more than a step, he was grasped by the arm and pulled out of the room.

"Fuck that. You are mine, and I am yours. You want a quick screw in the bathroom? Fine, I can do that."

Was he making a mistake by allowing this? Would he regret it later? His mind screamed yes, but his heart rejoiced and pushed for this connection. Gareth knew this wasn't the way things needed to be, but he was damned if he could stop the inevitable. He needed Zach more than he needed his next breath.

He glanced over his shoulder to make sure their quick exit hadn't caused a stir, but no one seemed to be paying attention to them. Gareth stopped resisting and gave in to Zach and his body's desperate need.

"Are you going to walk away from me again after this?" Gareth couldn't help the anger that filled his tone at the thought, but he needed to know now before things got too far. He had to prepare himself for what came next.

Zach didn't respond, just pulled Gareth in and shut the door and with a smirk, flipped the lock. "No more talking. This is what you wanted, isn't it? A quick fuck to ease the ache. A mindless screw to take the need away."

Zach continued talking as he stalked closer and closer to Gareth, slowly unbuckling his belt as he went.

"I want more than that with you. I want it all," Gareth said in a whisper of awe and need as he stood transfixed, watching Zach loosen his black dress pants.

"This is all you get. Take it or leave it, but speak now or forever hold your peace." Zach reached out and pushed Gareth against the wall. "This belongs to me, no one else," he said as he brushed the back of his hand over Gareth's straining cock. "See what I mean? Even your cock knows the truth." Zach smirked at the moan that escaped through Gareth's lips as he closed his eyes at Zach's touch.

"That's right, baby, relax and let me make us feel good." Zach leaned in and nuzzled against Gareth's neck as his hands undid the belt and opened Gareth's pants.

"Gods, I want to push you down over that sink and plunge balls deep, but I didn't come prepared." Both men sucked in a breath as Zach grasped both cocks and gave a slow pull. The friction from their cocks rubbing in his hand left Gareth panting for breath.

Zach groaned. "You want me to make you scream as I hold you down and plunge my aching cock in, don't you? You don't have to answer, your cock is leaking with every word out of my mouth. It's okay, babe, I want it, too."

Gareth didn't think he could talk if he wanted to. It took all he had to not come as Zach drove him slowly insane. Whimpers filled his ears and it took him a minute to realize they were coming from him.

"Oh, by the gods, baby, that feels good. Don't come yet, we don't want our suits getting dirty now, do we?"

Gareth's eyes flew open as Zach removed his hand from his throbbing cock. He stared into Zach's eyes as he slowly dropped to his knees and smiled up at Gareth.

"Don't worry, I won't let any get on your clothes." Zach winked and slid his tongue around the head of Gareth's cock head, lapping at the juices that flowed freely. "Delicious. Now do not scream. We don't need company."

Gareth didn't have time to process Zach's words before his mind blanked as wet heat engulfed him from root to tip. Holy fuck, Zach was deep throating him and that was the last conscious thought he had. Moans filled the room as Gareth fisted Zach's hair, urging him on. "Zach, I can't...I'm coming."

Instead of pulling off, Zach increased his suction as he slipped one hand to Gareth's balls and gave a slight squeeze at the same time his other hand reached back and rubbed lightly over Gareth's quivering hole. That was all it took, Gareth shuddered and came with a shout.

He couldn't move, his bones had liquefied. He pulled his head from the wall and stared down at the beautiful man at his feet.

"What happened to no screaming?" Zach said with a smirk.

"Sorry," Gareth blushed. "You didn't finish?"

Zach smiled, "Not yet." He stood and leaned against the opposite wall as he slowly stroked himself and watched as Gareth licked his lips. "You want a taste, don't you?"

He nodded, but once again found himself unable to speak coherently. Gareth pulled himself from the wall and moved closer to Zach. "Please."

"No, I don't think so." Gareth's eyes flew to Zach's in surprise. "You were going to let a stranger come in here and fuck you. Make you scream like I just did." Zach stopped talking and grunted as he reached over and grabbed a handful of paper towels from the dispenser. "Your ache has been taken care of, now I will take care of my own." With that, Zach came into the wad of towels.

Gareth felt his anger rise again at his words. How dare the ass treat him like this. "You really are a bastard, aren't you?"

"Not normally but what can I say, the gods bring out the worst in me. I don't trust any of you. You all meddle in people's lives like its nothing and then go on about your merry way. Who cares if the mortals suffer for your interference. You are gods, after all, and can do whatever you want."

Gareth watched as Zach cleaned himself up and walked out the door without looking back even once. The pain in his chest flared stronger than ever and he fell to his knees gasping for breath. He didn't need Thor to tell him, this time he knew it. His time was rapidly coming to an end.

Fifteen

Thor looked around in shock and disbelief. The mortals were going insane, that's all there was to it. He searched the room for Loki or Freyr for an explanation but neither were to be seen. Thor pushed his way through the undulating bodies on the dance floor and came to an abrupt stop.

"Freyr, what is going on? Why does it look like an orgy is about to break out any moment?" Thor demanded of the god.

"Well, you see I am a god of fertility and um, well, I might have gotten a little carried away." Freyr looked sheepish as he looked around at the havoc of the room. "This is why I haven't been to the mortal realm in a while. I forget sometimes and let my powers out to play a little strongly when I see something I want. It can affect others as you see."

Thor groaned in exasperation, "I forgot about that slight problem. The brothers are going to go nuts over this, they hate us gods as is. We really didn't need to give them any more ammunition."

"I don't think they all hate the gods. At least that one doesn't seem to hate Loki at the moment," Freya said as he pointed to a darkened alcove where Quentin was partly shielded from view by Loki's body.

"By the way his hands are gripping Loki's shirt, I would say he definitely doesn't hate him at the moment."

"Focus for a minute. How do we stop this before clothes start being removed and I screw this up even more than we already have?"

"I'll go, within a few minutes my effect should wear off and people will come to their senses. Sad day when a god wants to stop an orgy. What have we become?"

Thor didn't have time to answer before Freyr was gone and the sizzle that was running rampant through the room started to level out. He hadn't realized it was there until he felt it dissolving. The couples around him slowly melded back into causal dancing and the embracing couples glanced around in embarrassment to see who had caught them. Except for Loki and the brother, thankfully they were in a dark corner and not easily viewed. Thor walked up and cleared his throat to gain their attention.

"You two might want to cool it out in the open like this," Thor mumbled as he leaned against the wall to make it look less obvious.

"Fuck!" a soft voice called out in disbelief before Thor saw the brother Quentin take off at a rapid pace out of the hall.

"Why did you interrupt us? I finally got him to stay in the same room with me for five minutes and you scared him off," Loki complained.

"You might not have noticed but we have bigger problems."

"Yeah, tell me about it. I'm hard as hell and the only man I want just ran out on me. You are such a cock block, you know that?"

Thor rolled his eyes, "Zach and Gareth disappeared but from the looks on their faces when they did, it wasn't for a happily ever after. Not to mention we had the beginnings of a rather festive public orgy in progress a few short moments ago."

"Damn, I miss all the fun. It's been ages since I've been to a decent one."

"No, you were in the middle of it molesting the brother, if I don't miss my guess."

"I wasn't molesting him. He dragged me into the corner I will have you know." Loki smiled devilishly, "Can't rape the willing and all that."

"See if you can find Zach, I am going to find Gareth. Let's see how things went. With any luck I'm mistaken and I have righted one of the wrongs I did to this family."

Loki nodded and started to move away, mumbling just loud enough for Thor to hear, "What about the wrong you just did me, you cock blocking bastard."

***

Zach stormed from the benefit and headed to his car. The bastard gods hated him, that's the only conclusion he could come to.

Why would the fates give him his mate and make him a god? How cruel could they really be to one man?

"I've been looking all over for you. You just took off and I was worried," Jared called out as he trotted up to Zach.

"I'm fine, just not in the mood to talk."

"Bro, you aren't fine. I'm not blind or stupid. Talk to me."

"What do you want me to say?" Zach turned to face his brother. "The other half of my soul is up there right now and he is a fucking god. You know, those bastards who cursed our family, the ones that sat back and laughed as generations of our family were crucified and tortured for what they caused." Zach hung his head and sighed in defeat, "And the worst part is the only thing I want to do is go back up there and hold him close to me. To feel the comfort of his arms wrapped around me. To hear his voice tell me about his day and to see the smile that lights up the room when he sees me."

"You need to give him a chance. He isn't a full god, he isn't like them, and he is suffering as much and probably more."

Zach frowned as he rubbed at the building pain in his chest. His anger was slowly residing and the pain was overtaking it. "Jared, I..." Zach collapsed to the ground before he could finish his words.

"Shit!" Jared muttered as he reached out to catch his brother. He looked around desperately for help, but he didn't see anyone. "Come on, man, I need you to help me. I can't lift your heavy ass alone."

"Hold on. Let me help," a strong voice said from behind Jared as half the weight of his brother was taken.

"Thanks, man. I'm not sure where you came from but thank you. I couldn't hold him much longer." Jared glanced up at the man and was stunned speechless by the beauty that stood before him.

"Are you okay? You aren't going to drop too, are you?" the stranger asked with a chuckle as he watched Jared from the corner of his eye.

"What? No, sorry. I lost track of my thoughts for a minute there." Jared blushed. "Can you help me get him to our car over there?"

"Yeah, no problem." The two men carried Zach the short distance. "Can you hold him one second while I unlock the door?"

The stranger nodded and reached around to grab Zach fully. His arm brushed against Jared's body and flames erupted, sending chills down his body.

"Just hurry, please. I don't know how long I can hold him up." The words knocked Jared back to the present and he rushed to unlock and open the car door. The two men struggled but were finally able to get the unconscious body of Zach into the back seat.

Jared stepped back and shut the door. "I can't thank you enough for your help. I don't know what I would have done without you showing up like that."

The stranger smiled, "It was no problem. I hope your boyfriend is okay."

"Oh no, he's my brother, not my boyfriend," Jared quickly explained with a blush that made his face flame with embarrassment at his eagerness to set the record straight.

"Well now, that makes things a lot more interesting." The stranger offered his hand to a still stammering Jared. "I'm Riepal and it's a pleasure to meet you."

"Jared and the pleasure is definitely mine. I'm just glad you were here to help." Jared frowned and looked up at the taller man questioningly, "Just where did you come from though? I looked around and saw no one and then suddenly, there you were."

Riepal smiled enigmatically, "Let's just say I was…doing a flyby…saw you needed help and swooped in to assist."

Jared looked behind Riepal to see his brother, Quentin, approaching with a thunderous scowl on his face. "That's my other brother."

"Then I fear it's time to say farewell. With any luck I will see you around again sometime soon." With a slight bow, Riepal turned on his heel and disappeared into the darkness.

"Dude, you ready or not?" Quentin demanded from beside Jared.

"Yeah, yeah, no problem. Zach is down again, he is in the backseat," Jared called quietly as he searched the shadows for one last glance at the beautiful stranger.

***

The cold of the ground was seeping through the suit Gareth wore. The pain wasn't bearable and it definitely was not easing this time. Maybe this was the end, his soul had splintered and he was out of time.

"Gareth, can you hear me?" Thor said quietly as he crouched next to the figure on the bathroom floor.

"It hurts. So much worse than before. Please, I beg you, make it stop," Gareth cried out as tears fell freely down his pale face.

Thor placed a hand on his shoulder, "It's not done yet. We can still fix this, but time is running out."

"No offense, but I am not sure I can handle another one of your 'fixes', they tend to leave me on the ground writhing in pain."

"Bah, tiny mistake. Won't happen again. Let me think and we will fix this once and for all. In the meantime, hold on and I will get us back to your apartment and get you comfortable."

Before Gareth could blink, he was in his apartment, in his bed, naked and covered by the blankets. "For fuck's sake, you had to undress me, too?"

"To be honest, it wasn't like you weren't flashing me anyway. Just thought this would be more comfortable. Now lay back and let me see if I can ease the pain again." Thor reached out and touched Gareth's shoulder.

He wasn't sure what was supposed to happen, but he didn't feel anything. "Not helping yet," Gareth said between clenched jaws as a wave of intense pain shot through his chest.

"There. Sorry, the worse it gets, the harder it is to give you some relief."

Gareth sighed and relaxed back, exhausted from all that had transpired.

"I can't do another bout of being left behind like that. This one took me close, don't lie. I felt it rupture this time. One more time and it will be the end of me, and I assume him as well."

Thor nodded gravely, "Yes, you're right, it will. He won't let me get near him, but I will try to find out his condition and see if I can help alleviate some of the pain for him as well. His stubborn pride is killing you both."

Thor flashed from Gareth's side to Zach's house he shared with his brothers. He stayed hidden from view as he observed the brothers carrying the unconscious man into the house and to his bed.

"This is getting worse, I can feel it," Jared muttered.

Quentin nodded, lost in his own thoughts.

"Pay attention for two damn minutes, would you?" Jared demanded of his brother.

"What? I heard you. He is getting worse." Quentin paused and took a deep breath. "Call you-know-who but please let me leave the room first. I can't face him right now."

Thor frowned in puzzlement. Why would Quentin need to leave the room? What was going on with him? Things were not making any sense.

Jared nodded and waited for Quentin to escape before he sighed and threw his head back so he was staring at the ceiling. "Loki, you useless bastard. Get down here and answer some questions." He paused for a few heartbeats before trying again. "Quentin even says your name and you are here in a flash. Well guess what, you asshat, he's hiding from you. If you care about him like I think you might, get down here and help us."

Thor was stunned, when had this happened? How did the mere mortal see what he had failed to?

"Don't get lippy with me, boy. I was coming. What is it you need? Why is your brother hiding from me? And what makes you think I care for him anyway?" Loki grated out in a bored expression as he materialized next to Jared.

"Oh I don't know, maybe the fact that you practically stalk him and make innuendos at him until he runs blushing from the room. Or maybe because if he even whispers or thinks your name, you appear in the room. You may be blind to it, but I'm not." Jared scoffed at the ancient god. "Now, since you are here, help me with my brother. This brother," Jared said as he pointed to Zach laying in the bed.

"You need Thor for this, not me, goat boy," Loki snarled out in anger over Jared's accusations

"Fine, Thor, I need your help. Please, I know he hates you, but I don't know what else to do. Please come help us."

"What the fuck?! He gets please and I get called names and cursed at?" Loki said indignantly.

Thor couldn't help the chuckle that spilled from between his lips as he made his presence known in the room. "I'm here. I was coming to check on him, if I am honest."

Jared jumped at the god's words from behind him. "Why? How did you know?"

"Simple, Gareth is in much the same condition. Though he stays conscious." Thor stepped closer to the bed and laid a hand on Zach's shoulder. "Things are worse than I had realized. Zach is close to death. In fact, he is closer than Gareth."

"Close?" Jared's kneed buckled and he collapsed on the end of the bed, "How close is close?"

Thor contemplated how to answer before finally just shrugging, "It's hard to say. I can't see his soul, I can only feel it. He needs to stop pushing Gareth away, every time he does his soul cracks a bit farther."

"He is too stubborn to listen to reason. I tried talking to him about Gareth, but he ignores me or walks away. He has it in his head that Gareth is a god that uses people and interferes and destroys."

Loki gaped in shock, "Is that what you all think of us? No wonder your brother runs from me." He glanced around the room trying to process the latest revelation. "Please, tell him I'm sorry. I'll leave him alone, I never meant any harm."

Thor sighed, what a mess this night had become. He watched as Loki disappeared from the room and he turned back to Jared. "Give him a few days, I did what I could to make him comfortable. It won't work as well on him as he isn't a demi-god like Gareth. He will be up and moving soon, but I warn you if he walks away again, it will kill him and soon after, his soulmate as well.

Sixteen

The next week flew by in a haze for the brothers. It took Zach four days before he was up and mobile again. Quentin shuffled around the house, moping and irritable, and it took all Jared had to hold everything together. They had a group coming to the campgrounds in a little over an hour and he was running ragged trying to get all the last minute things arranged.

"Zach, they are arriving any minute. Have you found the campers list with the counselor names yet?" Jared asked in frustration as he watched Zach stare out the office window in thought. "Never mind. We can figure it out when they get here. Are you going to be able to help this week or not?"

Finally, with a huff, Jared stormed out of the office and left his brother to his thoughts.

Zach vaguely heard his brother, but he couldn't seem to dredge up enough energy to care. He couldn't get Gareth and what had transpired between them last weekend out of his mind. His mate fascinated him as no other ever had. He could admit he wanted him and not just for sex, but he just wasn't sure he could trust him. Gods were fickle and cruel.

A loud slam brought Zach from his thoughts and he turned to see Jared standing beside him. "They are here. Now get your ass out of that chair and come greet our guests. I can't do this alone." Jared turned and stormed out of the office, leaving Zach shocked and speechless.

He slowly climbed to his feet with a weary sigh and followed after his enraged little brother. In the hall, Quentin was waiting for him with a scowl. "What is wrong with Jared? He is in a foul ass mood."

Jared turned and stormed back to them, rage evident in his angry stride. "What's wrong with me? Did you seriously just ask me that? You two fucktards have done nothing but mope and stare off into space and it's only getting worse. I can't take much more of this. Zach, you have your head so far up your ass that you don't see what is right in front of you. You are rejecting the one man who was made just for you. You are literally dying because of it, but all you do is stare into space like that is going to fix anything." Zach sputtered but couldn't come up with a retort. Deep down he knew it was true. "And you, brother mine, are just as bad. Wake up and smell the coffee. Stop hiding and if nothing else, let the man show you a good time. When was the last time you had some fun?" The two men lowered their heads in shame as Jared once again stormed away, muttering under his breath.

"Let's go, we have campers to get settled and some issues to help resolve and standing in here having a pity party isn't going to help," Jared shot back as he pushed out the front door to meet the arriving buses.

Zach and Quentin shared a sheepish smile before following their youngest brother. "Never knew he had the balls to say shit like that," Quentin whispered.

"He takes after Mom more than I realized," Zach replied.

***

Zach stopped before the lead bus and waited for the home's director to descend.

This was one of his favorite parts of running the camp - seeing these kids' faces as they climbed off the bus with looks of distrust, apprehension, pain and anger and then seeing them leave a week later with smiles and sadness at it being over. Their lives sucked, but it was the least he and his brothers could do to give them a much needed escape from their everyday lives.

A tall, strikingly good-looking woman climbed off the bus and approached Zach. "Hi, I'm Marguerite. I run the center and I just wanted to say thank you for letting us come here on such short notice. Like I said on the phone the other day, the camp we had originally contacted fell through and I was so afraid I would have to cancel. These kids have been looking forward to getting away."

Zach smiled as the woman rambled and repeated most of what she had already told him on the phone a couple weeks earlier. "It's our pleasure. Let's get your kids unloaded and we can get everyone settled in cabins."

"That would be wonderful, it's been quite a day. One of our regular counselors had an emergency and couldn't be here. I had to call another in from vacation to cover. We are all looking forward to this week, I can assure you." Marguerite smiled and waved for the kids to disembark from the buses. "Kids, line up in two rows in front of your bus, we will get you all settled quickly into your cabins with a counselor and then the fun can begin."

The brothers smiled as the quiet of the camp was shattered with sounds of laughter, words and grunts as the kids jostled for position.

"Hey, gang. My name is Zach, these are my brothers, Quentin and Jared. Welcome to Camp Kid. If you guys will give us five minutes, we can get you all settled in.

"Don't grumble, if you can wait patiently we will have a campfire tonight and we can roast marshmallows and stuff." Zach smiled as the kids shifted anxiously from foot to foot as he spoke. "Sound like a deal?"

A chorus of 'Yeah' and 'Yes' filled the air.

"Marguerite, we can't seem to find the list of how many campers you have nor who your counselors are. Without that, we weren't able to split the kids up among the cabins," Jared piped in as he shot a glare at Zach.

"That's quite all right. At the moment, I have five counselors and twenty-seven kids, including me. A sixth counselor is on his way, but since it was last minute he wasn't able to make it to ride the bus with us."

Zach nodded, "Perfect. We can do the six cabins closest to the mess hall and the activities. Would you like to split the kids up?"

"Sure, that would probably be easiest." Marguerite smiled and called the remaining four counselors over. "Each of you are going to be in charge of five or six kids."

"You will all be given a cabin that is identified by color of the paint and the animal on the flag that flies from the top," Jared added as Marguerite took a breath.

Zach supplied a cabin name and waited as she assigned a counselor and a group of kids to it before giving the next name.

"We have five kids left, but their counselor isn't here yet," Marguerite said as shit bit her lip in worry.

"If they don't mind, I can be their counselor till the real one arrives," Jared said in a rush of excitement.

"That would be lovely, thank you." Marguerite called over the five kids and introduced them to Jared. "He is going to be your counselor until Mr. G arrives. You will be in the…" She paused and looked at Zach for the answer.

"Oh, sorry. The Red Phoenix cabin," he supplied as the kids whooped and hollered their excitement.

"Come on, gang, let's go get settled in. There is so much to do, you guys will be begging for this week to never end." Jared winked and led his campers away.

"That's my cue I think. I have to get my kids set up as well." Marguerite called her group forward and headed off.

Zach turned to look at Quentin. "So…"

Quentin shrugged and stared off in the direction Jared had just gone. "Guess I will get things set up for the roast tonight. You wanna check the firewood and get the pit ready?"

Zach nodded, "Yeah, sounds like a plan."

***

The long winding road through the woods calmed Gareth, as nothing else had been able to accomplish it over the last week. Being called in to work, as much as it sucked since he was on vacation, might have been the best thing to happen for him. Besides, he was going to be camping in the woods, close to nature. He was getting the best of both worlds.

He pulled up next to the main building and turned off his car. Camp Kid looked just like he would expect a camp to look like. Guess the movies got one thing right in this instance. He climbed out of the car and stretched, feeling the soothing presence of the wilderness fill him and soothe the never-ending urge to be with nature.

Gareth walked to the main office and rapped on the door. After a few minutes, he gave up and walked down the couple of steps to look around. Someone had to be close by to give him directions to his cabin to unload.

A curse from the blue cabin to the right drew his attention. He didn't see anyone, so he called out. "Anyone here?"

"Yeah, inside," a vaguely familiar voice called out. Gareth couldn't hear the voice well enough to place it, for some reason it was muffled and garbled. He climbed the three steps and entered the dim cabin. Gareth frowned and looked around in puzzlement. "Hello?"

"Back here," the voice answered. "Don't let the door...shut," the voice called just as the door slammed of its own accord.

"Shit, sorry. It kinda closed on its own," Gareth said as he turned and pulled on the door handle. "What the fuck?" Gareth mumbled as he pulled harder on the handle.

"The door gets stuck. It's why we leave it open," the voice said as it drew closer.

Gareth froze as he finally recognized the voice he should have known. His body had been trying to tell him his mate was close, but he had been too preoccupied to pay attention. He turned slowly and faced the man who kept rejecting him.

"What are you doing here?" Gareth asked in bewilderment.

"That's a better question for you. My brothers and I own this place. What are you doing here?" Zach demanded in shock.

"I'm a counselor with the group here this week," Gareth trailed off as he laughed in spite of himself. "I swear if I didn't know better, I would think the gods had a hand in this, but since all their endeavors end up backfiring, this has to be a major coincidence."

"I don't believe in coincidence. Are you sure this wasn't set up by one of your brethren?"

Gareth shook his head, "No, I was on vacation and wasn't even supposed to be at this camp. It was a last minute request when one of the others had to leave town for a family emergency."

Zach sighed and sat down on one of the empty cots. "Might as well get comfy, we could be here awhile."

"Why is that?" Gareth asked in confusion.

"Cause no one knows I am here. We don't use this cabin except for storage for the winter. No one has reason to come to this cabin to look for me. I just happened to come in because the axe I was using to chop fire wood broke and I knew we had an old one in storage."

"Won't one of your brothers come looking for you? Surely they will need you for something before long. You run this camp after all."

"Nope, when I was done I told them I was going to get cleaned up and run into town for a few necessities and that I would get dinner while there."

"What about my car, won't someone notice it and wonder who it belongs to?"

"That's a possibility, but the cabins your kids are in are down the road a bit. They really don't have reason to come up here considering all the events are happening down there and even our house is down that way."

"Well, fuck. What about my group of kids I am the counselor for? What's happening with them?"

"Jared." Zach sighed and rubbed his hands down his face in frustration. Being this close to the man who had been slowly driving him insane all week was playing havoc on his body. "He volunteered to be acting counselor till you arrived. Marguerite wasn't sure when you would show up after all."

The two men lapsed into silence as they took turns trying not to look at the other. Zach couldn't deny the pull he felt in his gut to get close to his man, but his head still screamed to be cautious.

"How did you become a counselor for a youth home?"

"It's a long story. You sure you want to hear it?" Gareth asked in a low tone.

Zach nodded and leaned forward, as if to make sure he could hear every word out of Gareth's mouth.

"I grew up in one, not a good one either. When I become an adult, I knew I wanted to give back and help kids have a better beginning then I did."

"How in the hell did a god grow up in an orphanage?

"I'm not sure who told you I was a god, but I can assure you I am only half. My father was a troll my goddess of a mother fell for. She got pregnant and left me to my father to raise. He died when I was a toddler, the state sent me to a home and that's where I lived until I turned 15 and ran away. I went to that cave where you found me and lived there for the next couple of years."

Gareth sighed and moved to lean against the wall so he could stare out the window at the woods that called to him. "One day my mom showed up. She had been unable to come to me due to some errand she had been on for Odin. I stayed in that cave until I thought I would go mad from lack of human contact." Gareth laughed in self-deprecation. "It's forever my curse to long for the solitude of the woods, caves and mountains while in the city and crave the city when I'm in the wilderness."

Zach didn't say anything in response, he couldn't as his mind whirled with the things he had just learned. Gareth wasn't what he thought at all. "How long have you been working with the kids?"

"About fifteen years now. I know you thought I was like the gods, but I grew up here like a mortal human being. I know nothing of their ways, and if I am to be honest, I only tolerate them. They took my mother away for seventeen years and left me to live in that forsaken home of pain and loneliness. I vowed one day to do my best to help kids like me and give them something to hold on to, something that would make them want to be better. I live in a crappy apartment with nothing, because every waking moment I am either in my cave or with those kids. Every dime I make is spent on getting them things they need or the home needs."

Zach slowly stood and approached Gareth. "I'm sorry I judged you. I felt the god power in you and I reacted without giving you a chance. I've treated you like shit and walked out on you after grinding your feelings into the ground. You have every right to hate me, and you should. I hate myself right now. Jared kept telling me that I had you wrong, but I let my anger and hatred for the curse placed upon my family by Thor cloud my judgement."

"I didn't try real hard to convince you of who I was either. I let my hormones dictate my actions. I saw you and that was the end. My brain short-circuited and my blood rushed to my cock."

"Are you saying that isn't the case anymore?"

"Fuck no, I'm so hard one touch and I will come all over the place. At the same time, I am tired of being rejected and pushed away. There is only so much rejection a man can take, and that counts double for when it's the other half of his soul doing it."

Zach reached up and gently turned Gareth's face toward him. "What if I told you I am tired of fighting this? What if I said just hearing your voice makes me feel like I could fly? That thoughts of you have filled my head nonstop since I left you in that cave.

"I feared to believe you could be different and I let my prejudice influence me. The truth is I crave you. Not just your body, but your mind, your heart and your soul. I need you like the trees need water. You are what makes me whole, makes me feel."

Gareth swallowed and closed his eyes in fear. Did he dare believe Zach had changed this much so quickly? How could he believe him? If Zach left he would die, he knew it as surely as he knew the sky was blue.

"I don't know if I can take the chance of you walking away again," Gareth whispered in a pained voice.

"You know I won't, I can't. If I do we both die, but it's more than that and you know it. My heart, body and soul belong to you. I let my mind cloud things but over the last few hours, I have come to know the truth. I'm miserable without you. I need you in my life. I would rather die right now than ever hurt you again."

Gareth felt a rush of something pulse through his body as he gave into what they both desperately wanted. Zach was right, they didn't have a choice. They were two halves of a whole and without the other, life was dark and dreary. The few minutes he had with Zach in that bathroom had shown him how lonely and sad life was without him. He was alive but lived as if he was dead. Zach was his breath, his heartbeat and his soul.

Seventeen

"Please, don't walk away this time," Gareth whispered as he moved in to kiss Zach for the first time in their short relationship.

Their lips met in a bone-melting kiss so hot, it could melt the polar ice caps. Zach's groan filled Gareth's ears as he deepened the kiss and pushed Gareth against the wall.

"Baby, I need you...so bad. I...can't be...gentle...this time. I need...you too badly...to wait," Zach said in between kisses.

"Take me, I'm yours to command."

"You like it when I take control? Tell you what to do?"

"Yes, I love it. It's a turn on and makes me feel completely dependent on you. You're in control of my pleasure. Just the idea makes me ready to come." Gareth groaned, "Please, I want you so bad." Before he could utter another word, Zach turned them around and walked him back toward one of the cots. Their mouths fused together as they ripped at each other's clothes in a frenzied passion that left them both breathless and panting.

"Slow down, let me look at you," Gareth pleaded as Zach pushed him closer to the bed. Gareth gasped as Zach lowered his pants and rubbed against him.

"Feeling is so much better, my love."

Gareth spun and pushed Zach to sit on the bed. "My turn. I want a taste of what I was denied last weekend." He sank to his knees and spread Zach's legs apart.

"Fuck my mouth, but don't come. I want you inside of me for that."

Zach sputtered at his words, but all rational thought evaporated the moment he felt Gareth's mouth engulf him. Zach bucked his hips and let out a guttural cry. "Holy gods."

Gareth pulled back so only Zach's tip was still in his mouth. "Do it, baby. Fist your hands in my hair and fuck my mouth."

Zach didn't need to be told twice, the feel of all that wet heat wrapped around his cock was driving him insane. He lifted his hips and thrust up as he pulled Gareth's head down farther on his cock, over and over, until he was seeing stars. Gareth hummed and sucked harder the faster Zach pumped into him.

"Stop, I'm too close," Zach panted as he pulled Gareth off. "You are so damn sexy." Zach pulled Gareth up for a scorching kiss. He could taste himself on his tongue and it lit fires through this body.

"You ready for this? I don't have any lube, but I promise to make sure you are ready before I do anything."

"It's okay. Just fuck me, I like the pain. It won't take much for me to be ready."

Zach grunted and stood up, "Strip now."

Gareth smiled and climbed to his feet. He loved when Zach got demanding like that. It made his blood boil and his body burn for more. He wanted, no, needed to be possessed and marked by his mate.

Gareth stepped back and slowly removed his pants. Zach licked his lips as he saw Gareth's cock leaking precum. Gareth smiled and stroked his cock for Zach's pleasure. "You gonna fuck me and make me scream your name? Going to make me feel it and know who I belong to?"

Zach's cock twitched at his words. "You already know that you belong to me. It's okay because I belong to you, too." Zach stepped forward and gripped Gareth's wrist. "Stop. I didn't say you could touch yourself like that." Gareth whimpered and removed his hand.

"Yes, Sir."

"Good boy, now go lean over that table and spread your legs. Don't move from that position until I tell you. Understood?"

Gareth nodded and rushed to do what he was bid. By the gods, this man really was perfect for him in every way.

Zach followed and brushed his hand down Gareth's back, over one cheek and between his legs to fondle his aching balls.

"That's it. I've got you. Just relax and feel," Zach whispered as he brought his other hand up to massage gently at Gareth's other cheek. "Reach back here and spread yourself for me. I find myself hungry for a taste of you."

Gareth whimpered and precum dripped and made a small puddle on the floor. He slowly brought his arms behind himself and did as he was he told. He was rewarded with a long slow lap of a hot tongue over his spasming hole.

"That's right, baby. You taste so good," Zach whispered as he buried his face and rolled his tongue, stabbing and flicking as he fondled Gareth's balls with his hand.

Gareth couldn't speak, all he could do was whimper and cry out in ecstasy as he was brought closer and closer to the edge. "Sir, please. I need more."

Zach smiled and leaned back. "Begging, I like that," he said as he placed one finger against the tight bud and lightly tapped, as if asking for permission to enter.

"Gods, please. Yes," Gareth mumbled as he gripped his cheeks tighter.

"How do I know you are ready for me?" Zach asked as he pulled his finger away and sucked on it to get it as wet as he could. His mate might like pain, but he had to make sure to make this was as easy as he could without lube.

"Please. I need you so bad," Gareth cried out as he wiggled on the table.

"Don't move. I already told you that," Zach growled as he inserted one finger up to his first knuckle. Gareth's whimpers filled the room. "Like that, do you?" Zach asked as he slipped it in farther and then pulled all the way out.

"No, don't stop," Gareth demanded.

"I'm not stopping, baby. I wouldn't do that to either of us." Zach reached around with his hand and stroked Gareth's cock as he inserted his finger back into his quivering hole. "That's it, baby, suck my finger in. Gods, you are so hot." Zach sucked in a breath at the tight heat that pulled at him.

"More, please, I need more."

Zach was happy to oblige. He was too close to the edge to wait much longer. He pushed a second and then third finger in and thrust as he stroked Gareth's cock. The whimpers and cries of lust grew louder as Zach scissored his fingers, preparing him the best he could. He pulled back and replaced his fingers with his cock. "You ready for this, love?"

A guttural groan and a nod was all the response Gareth was able to give. Zach took that as permission and slowly pushed himself deep.

"Fuck, baby. You are so tight. You are squeezing me like a vise." Zach panted as he slowly pulled out and pushed back in deeper.

"Harder. Now. Harder, please."

Zach wasn't sure he could wait so he did as Gareth asked and pushed all the way in and pulled out until only his tip was still inside. "Hold on to the table, baby. I'm going to make you scream now."

As soon as Gareth did as instructed, Zach rammed himself back in and started thrusting for all he was worth. Sweat beaded and fell down his face as he raced for the pinnacle that was just out of reach. Gareth arched and pushed back into every stroke as if his life depended on it. Words were gone, there was nothing left but the aching need they had for each other. Gareth stiffened and let out a yell. "Right there. Yes, that's the spot, right there," he said as he shuddered and shook in Zach's arms.

"Baby, I can't last much longer," Zach whispered as he rammed in harder with every whimper out of Gareth's mouth. A guttural scream filled the room as Gareth came. He collapsed on the table with a contented smile on his face. "Almost there. Yes, that's it," Zach cried as he followed after and fell on top of his mate.

Minutes passed slowly as the two men came back to themselves. "Hold on, baby, I'm going to pull out. Then we can move to one of the cots and be comfortable."

Gareth nodded, but words were still too much for him. He winced at the feeling of emptiness as Zach pulled away.

"Hold on, we can use my under shirt to clean up a bit," Zach said as he leaned down and kissed Gareth.

Minutes later, they were dressed and laying on a cot on their sides facing each other. "I'm sorry for doubting you and not giving you a chance. I won't, no, I can't let you go now. We belong together in every way there is," Zach whispered.

"I wouldn't let you. My soul is complete, the world has color all because I have you," Gareth replied.

Eighteen

Thor stopped outside the blue cabin and glanced to the brothers who stood beside him. "I think it's safe now."

"Why didn't we think of locking them together somewhere?" Loki complained as he stared at the door.

Quentin glanced at Loki with a quizzical look. The god hadn't made one comment, suggestive or otherwise, since they had shown up ten minutes ago. For that matter, Loki hadn't even looked at him. Quentin had spent weeks avoiding and running from the god, this is what he wanted…wasn't it?

"Just knock so they know we are coming in," Jared laughingly joked.

"We can hear you, you know. Asshats," Gareth grumbled through the door. The group assembled outside, chuckled and then opened the door.

"I see everything worked out for the best. Loki, we did good, my friend." Gareth and Zach rolled their eyes before stepping out of the cabin.

"Yeah, you did real well," Jared said as he walked away, mumbling loud enough for them all to hear, "Just skip me when it's my turn, if you don't mind. I could do without your brand of matchmaking."

Thor rolled his eyes and ignored him. "So you guys are happy? No pain, right? No more hating us for the curse?" he asked hopefully.

"Yes, we are happy. I don't hurt at all, and I can't say I don't hate you, but my brothers are right. Without the curse, we wouldn't have been able to save as many people as we have.

"I've known that for a long time but truth be told, it was easier to hold on to my anger than to admit that it's not so bad," Zach said with a wink to Gareth.

"I don't have any pain any longer either. I only feel happiness and love."

Thor placed a hand on each of their shoulders and waited. A slow smile filled his face. "Good news, my boys. Your souls are mended and you have bonded."

Thor turned to Quentin. "You're next. Ready or not." Thor had to hide a smile as he saw Loki and Quentin frown at his words. This was going to be so much fun.

He turned back to Gareth and Zach, "By the way, when you bonded, you activated all your god powers, Gareth. That includes immortality and by mating Zach, that extended to him. The fates aren't that cruel to deny you your love by him dying."

Thor laughed at their shocked expression as he faded away to go tell his wife the good news. His soul was lighter; he had one down and two to go.

About the Author

Hi, I'm Sheri Lyn. I live in Florida with the love of my life, my dog Koda a Corgi/Dwarf Chow mix. I love living here and couldn't imagine living anywhere else.

I just started my journey into the indie book world. I have books in several genres in the works. I'm an avid reader who kept dreaming of a story that wanted to be told and that's where my first book was born.

When I'm not reading or proofing, I'm at the evil day job where my sanity is tested on a daily basis. My sarcastic quips can provide a much-needed break until I can return home to Koda and books, my two joys.

Please visit my website to keep up with my books and to sign up for my newsletter for excerpts, giveaways and fun.

Sherilynauthor.com
Twitter - @sherilynauthor

Made in the USA
Charleston, SC
08 July 2016